# My Cat Ate My Homework

David Blaze

This book is a work of fiction. Names, characters, places, and incidents are the product of the author's imagination or are used factiously. Any resemblance to actual events, locales, or persons, living or dead, is coincidental.

# For Zander...

## Wow! That's Awesome!

# CONTENTS

# THURSDAY MORNING

I didn't know the answer to Miss Turner's math question when she tapped on my desk. I smiled, swallowed hard, and shrugged my shoulders. I wanted to run out of the classroom and go home.

"Does anyone else know the answer?" she asked all the kids around me. She was the youngest teacher at the school and had a pretty smile with bright white teeth. I wished I could smile back. I stared down at my desk. I was good at every subject but math. I hated it.

Jennifer stood up behind me. Of course she knew the answer. She was the president of the Mathletes, the school math team. She only wore blue dresses like every day was a tea party. She had matching blue ribbons in her blond hair. "I do, Miss Turner," she said. I didn't have to turn around to see her glaring at me. "The answer is four. Everyone knows that. Well, almost everyone."

The other three girls around me laughed. They were all on the math team. Jennifer's math army surrounded me.

"Everyone settle down," Miss Turner said. She leaned in close to my ear and whispered, "Melissa, meet me at my desk after class." I didn't know if I was in trouble or not. I sank into my chair.

She stood at the front of the classroom and faced all eighteen of us. "I hope you've all had a chance to work on your math assignment. It's due tomorrow."

I felt like a deer caught in headlights. The assignment had been given to us weeks earlier. I hadn't even started on it. I thought I had a lot of time to figure it out and get it done. But now it was due tomorrow and I had no idea how to do it!

The class bell rang. I sat at my desk as the rest of the kids walked past me. Jennifer and her math army stopped in front of my desk. "We're competing in the county math championship tomorrow night. You should come watch us win." She flipped her hair back and snapped her fingers for her army to follow her out. "Maybe you can learn something. But I doubt it."

I knew she was being mean, but my daddy had taught me to be nice to everyone. "I hope you win."

Amanda stayed at my desk when the other girls walked away laughing. She was the only girl on the math team who was nice to me. She wore big glasses and dressed like we had a school uniform. "Don't listen to her. She's having a bad hair day." We both chuckled.

"Amanda, let's go," Jennifer commanded. Amanda smiled at me then joined the rest of her team by the door. The other girls kept pointing at me. They whispered to each other and laughed. One of the girls laughed so hard that she coughed and couldn't stop. I felt small.

"Are you okay, Vanessa?" Miss Turner asked her. "That's a nasty cough." She rushed over to Vanessa.

"I'm fine," she said, still coughing. "It's only a cold."

Miss Turner stood by Vanessa's side and put a hand on her forehead. "You're burning up. Go see the school nurse." She looked at her watch. "I've got to head that direction for a minute. I'll go with you."

I hoped she was okay, but I was glad I didn't have to talk to Miss Turner now. I hadn't started on the math assignment and wouldn't get it done by tomorrow. I'd have to stay home and hide under my bed all day.

"I'll be right back," she said to Vanessa. "I need to talk to Melissa."

She marched to my desk and stood over me. "I know you're having a hard time in this class. Let's get you some extra help." She put a hand on my shoulder. "I'll talk to your dad."

I smiled at her as she walked out of the room with Vanessa. I missed my dad. I wished I knew when he was coming home. He was an electrician. He went to Puerto Rico to help them get their electricity back after Hurricane Irma took it away. He was like a superhero.

I stood and put my math book in my backpack. One other person could help me. He had blue eyes and was the smartest person I knew. He was my friend Joe.

# THURSDAY AFTERNOON

I headed straight for Joe's house when I got off the school bus. He lived on the street next to mine. We used to hang out after school together, but he was never around anymore. He was always with Shane. It was super weird because Shane used to be the school bully. He was eleven years old like Joe and me, but he was so tall that he looked like he was supposed to be in high school.

I stared at the yard before I walked into it. Patches of grass and patches of dirt filled the yard. The house was older than my dad. A chicken coop was in the backyard. Joe's great grandma Rita had lived here for a long time. He and his mom moved in last year.

I brushed my hair back with my fingers and straightened my clothes before I knocked on the door. I smiled as the door opened. I hoped Joe was on the other side.

"Joe's not here," his little cousin Dana said with her arms crossed after she opened the door. She had beautiful bright brown hair. She didn't live here but spent a lot of time with Joe and his mom. She was a tough kid and took karate lessons, but she was nice if you were nice to her.

"Where's he at?" I asked her. "I need his help." I felt desperate. My dad helped me when he was home. My sister was supposed to be taking care of me, but she was in college and always busy. Joe was my last hope in getting the math assignment done.

"I don't know," she said, shrugging her shoulders.

I wanted to cry. Dana was seven years old. I couldn't ask her for help. "Can I talk to your aunt?" Miss Johnson was an adult. She could help me.

"She'll be back in a minute," Dana explained. "She went across the street to ask Mrs. Hunter something. You can hang out here if you want. I have pizza rolls." She paused. "But they're mine. Don't touch them."

"Come and get em!" a high-pitched voice shouted from behind her. "Pizza rolls for everyone!" My favorite cat in the world, Peanut Butter Jelly, poked his head out from between Dana's legs. He was laughing his head off.

I laughed with the talking tiger striped orange tabby. The brown stripes on his orange fur were beautiful. His blue eyes appeared green in the right light. It was hard to believe he'd only been here for a few weeks. It was harder to believe he could talk like you and me.

"Those are my pizza rolls!" Dana complained.

"They were," Peanut Butter Jelly said, standing on his hind legs and rubbing his belly. "They were nice and warm going down my throat. Now they're safe in my belly."

"What!" Dana shouted. She brushed him out of the way and marched back into the house. "This better be a joke!"

Peanut Butter Jelly looked up at me and whispered, "April fools."

I shook my head and laughed. "It's not April, Peanut Butter Jelly." It was February. He had learned so much from us since the first day he stood up and talked. I had always wanted a cat. I wished he could live with me. PJ was independent, but he was okay with me calling him my cat.

"Maybe it's not April," he said, "but it should be." He winked at me. "And don't call me Peanut Butter Jelly anymore. I'm not a little kitten." He puffed his chest out. "I've got hair on my chest. Call me PJ."

I was confused. "You have hair on your entire body."

Dana stormed back over to us. "That wasn't funny." She had a plate full of pizza rolls in her hand. She shoved the plate in front of me. "Hold this. But don't touch my pizza rolls. Don't you dare touch them." I didn't argue with her. It was useless. I didn't want the pizza rolls anyways.

Dana reached into her pocket and pulled out a metal pen. It looked like the one Miss Cox had in her English class. She called it a laser pointer. Whenever she pointed it at the chalkboard, a small red ball of light would appear.

"I've got something for you," she said to PJ. She pressed the button on the end of the pen and pointed the pen at a wall in the living room. A red ball of light appeared on the wall.

PJ faced the wall and got down on all four paws. His tail waved back and forth slowly. "We meet again, evil red ball. I will defeat you." He didn't realize Dana was controlling the light with her pen. And that it wasn't evil.

Dana waved the pen back and forth. The red light moved from one side of the wall to the other. PJ's head moved in rhythm with it. His tail waved faster and faster. He lifted his rear end into the air like he was ready to attack.

"You can run but you can't hide," PJ mumbled. "It's go

time!" He raced toward the wall like a wild animal. He jumped up and swatted at the red light when he reached the wall. It moved faster than him. Side to side. He kept swatting at it like a crazy cat.

I burst out laughing. There was no way for him to catch the ball of light. Dana smirked at me and yawned as she waved the pen one last time. Then she pressed the button on her pen again. The ball of light disappeared.

PJ spun in circles. "Not again! I will find you. And I will win." He ran from room to room. "Why does this keep happening to me?" he yelled.

Dana closed the door behind us. "That should keep him busy for a few hours." She snatched the plate of pizza rolls back from me. "Come help me feed the chickens." She headed for the kitchen. The back door was in there.

I set my backpack down on a dining room chair. I opened the backpack and pulled out my math book. I laid the book on the table so Miss Johnson would see it when she came home.

The three-page math assignment was stuffed in the middle of my book. Miss Turner called it an assignment, but it was really a math test. And it was worth half of the grade for that class. If I failed the assignment, then I would fail the class. That's why I was desperate.

"Hurry up," Dana commanded. For a little kid, she sure was bossy. She set her plate of pizza rolls on the kitchen counter. Then she opened the back door and waited for me to join her. I shook my head and followed her out the door. She shoved a bag of chicken feed into my hands as soon as we stepped outside.

"Last person out the door feeds the chickens," she said. She marched toward the chicken coop. I sighed and followed her past the outhouse. I chuckled when I remembered the first time Joe opened it. He ran away screaming after a grasshopper jumped out at him.

We stopped at the chicken coop. Five chickens were walking around the fenced area. The rest were inside.

"We don't have all day," Dana complained. She pointed at the bag of chicken feed and nodded at the chickens. "Hurry up."

I threw out a handful of feed. More chickens came out of the coop. "I miss him," I said to Dana.

She put her hands in her pockets. "Who?"

I missed my best friend. "Joe." I couldn't look at her. I felt lost without him. I passed him in the halls at school sometimes. He didn't talk to me like he used to.

Dana huffed. "Me too. He's different since Fox left." PJ wasn't the first animal to talk on this land. Fox left weeks ago to return to his parents. Joe was heartbroken about it. Fox had been his best friend.

"Most nights," Dana continued, "he sits out here and stares into the woods." I hated to hear that.

Dana sat on the grass and folded her legs. She took a deep breath and closed her eyes. She became calm and still, like she was in another world. I thought it was weird but didn't say anything. I wondered what she was learning in the karate class.

She missed Fox as much as her cousin Joe did. "Let's go back inside," she said after a minute. "Hopefully PJ didn't burn the house down."

I smiled and walked with her back into the house. I froze when I saw the kitchen table. My math book was wide open, and the three-page assignment was spread over the table. What had PJ done? "No, no, no, no, no." I was sure he had destroyed it in his search for the red ball of light.

I ran to the table and grabbed the papers. They were

okay. I breathed a sigh of relief and opened my backpack again. The math book and papers would have to stay in there until Miss Johnson came home. One of the papers caught my attention.

"What is this?" I whispered.

Dana sat at the table and stuffed another pizza roll into her mouth. "It's a sheet of paper." She winked at me when I glanced up. I held the paper in front of me and looked over the other two sheets. Every math problem had an answer next to it – even the bonus question about seconds, minutes, and hours on a clock. Someone had filled in the blanks.

"Where's it at?" PJ asked when he raced into the kitchen. "I will catch that red ball. It can't hide forever." He looked beneath the table and opened all the cabinets.

It felt foolish, but I had to ask him. "Did you do this?" I held the homework out to him.

He stood on his hind legs and looked at the papers. "The math game? It wasn't very fun." He held his paws out. "No one wins."

I didn't think I could trust his answers to be right. Dana agreed with me. "What do you know about math? You chase a ball of light and think you're going to catch it."

"I'll catch it," PJ promised. "Wait and see." He motioned to me. "Cats know everything about math. We have to know how high to jump. How fast to run. And how many naps to take."

I had no idea if the answers were right, but this was a talking cat. How many cats can talk? Maybe, just maybe PJ was a math genius.

"Twenty," Dana said, laughing. "You take twenty naps a day. You're so lazy."

I put the math book and papers into my backpack and zipped it closed. It would take most kids hours, or even days, to do the math work PJ had done. Or in my case — forever. I wasn't sure what to do.

"My aunt will be home soon," Dana reminded me.

My heart was racing. Was it crazy to think I could turn these papers in to Miss Turner tomorrow? They were already done. No one would ever have to know a cat had done the work.

"I'm going home," I told Dana. "My sister is waiting for me." That wasn't true. My sister never waited for me. She was out with her friends.

"Okay," Dana said. "I'll let Joe know you were here. Kissy, kissy." I blushed. Dana knew I liked Joe. I hung out at this house way too much.

"Bye, Melissa," PJ said. "Call me if you find that ball of light."

As I walked home, I couldn't stop sweating. I felt

excited and guilty about the idea of turning in the math papers. I had never cheated in my life, but I was about to fail that class. Maybe PJ was the answer to all my problems.

# LATE THURSDAY AFTERNOON

I set my backpack on my bed when I got home. My sister Angie wasn't there yet. I hoped she'd come home soon because I needed her advice. She was eight years older than me. She'd know what to do.

I sat on my bed and stared at the backpack. Tomorrow morning, I could open it in class and hand the math assignment to Miss Turner. The answers were probably wrong but at least she'd think I tried. I didn't want her to be disappointed in me.

The only other thing I could do was tell Miss Turner I didn't do the assignment. If I admitted that, I'd fail the class. She'd call my dad when he came back from Puerto Rico and have a meeting with him. I'd have to go to summer school. My life would be over.

I heard Angie's old car pull into the driveway. I raced into the living room and waited by the front door. My big sister had been in Miss Turner's class years ago. She'd know what to do.

"Hey, sis," Angie said when she walked in. "I've got a date tonight and I need to get ready." She wore a cute pink dress.

I stood in front of her so she couldn't get around me. She would lock herself in the bathroom for hours doing her hair and putting on makeup. "I need your help."

She sighed. "What is it?"

I raced into my bedroom, unzipped my backpack, and pulled the assignment out of my math book. Angie was standing in front of me when I turned around. I handed the papers to her.

"What's this?" She shuffled the three pages. "I remember this stuff. I was never any good at it."

I guess it ran in our genes. "Me either. A cat did it for me." She had never met PJ. I wasn't sure how she'd react.

Angie stared at me. I didn't know what she'd say next. She didn't say anything. She burst out laughing. "Whatever you say." She looked back down at the papers. "This looks good. It's better than I could have done." She handed the papers back to me. "I'm proud of you."

I was speechless. My sister had never been proud of me. She usually called me names or ignored me. It felt wrong that she was proud of me for something I didn't do.

"Are you okay, sis?" she asked. "What do you need help with?"

I sat on my bed. I wanted to tell her the truth. I wanted to tell her that PJ could walk and talk. I wanted to tell her that I was like her and couldn't understand the math homework. But I realized I couldn't.

I laughed when I wondered what would happen if she believed a cat had done my homework. She'd put me in a home for crazy people. Everyone knows cats can't do homework. They can't even talk.

"Everything's fine," I told her. "You should get ready for your date." She smiled and walked out of the bedroom.

I put my backpack on the floor and laid back on my bed. I had no idea what to do. I mean, I knew what the right thing was. But was the right thing the best thing? Why did life have to be so hard? I wished I was an adult.

I almost convinced myself to get up and tell Angie that I was there the night PJ stood and talked for the first time. There was something magical about the land Joe's great grandma had left for him and his mom.

I yawned as the room got darker. I closed my eyes and tried to figure out what I was going to do tomorrow. My stomach felt like it was twisted inside and out. I wanted to do the right thing. I wasn't sure if I could.

# FRIDAY MORNING

I was the last person off the school bus that morning. I felt sick when I thought about walking into Miss Turner's class. I didn't want to get out of my seat. The bus driver stared at me through his rearview mirror. I knew he wanted me to get out of my seat. He had a big frown on his face.

I took a deep breath, stood, and picked my backpack up from the floor. It felt like it weighed a thousand pounds. I slid it onto my back and walked slowly off the bus. Daddy had taught me to smile when I felt sad. I'm not sure it did any good.

I felt invisible as the kids around me went into the school. Some of them were excited and didn't stop talking. Some of them bumped into me and kept going without saying a word. Some of them looked as sick as I felt.

I passed by the gym and saw Coach Brown yelling at a kid. He always wore a red cap and had a whistle around his neck. I don't think he liked kids. Most of us were afraid of him.

Before I reached Miss Turner's room, Jennifer stepped in front of me. "Hey, Melissa," she said in a sweet tone. Her math army wasn't complete. Tracy and Amanda were with her, but Vanessa wasn't. "You have a great smile."

I wasn't sure why she was being nice. She had been mean to me ever since the second grade. "Thank you," I told her. "I love your hair."

She turned to Tracy and laughed. "Doesn't she have a great smile?"

"Sure," Tracy said. "If you count her pretty teeth, that's the number of times she'll have to take sixth grade math class before she passes it." They both laughed at me and walked away. Amanda whispered, "Sorry." I wanted to get back on the school bus.

I stepped into Miss Turner's class with my head down. I knew what I had to do. I sat at my desk and set my backpack on the floor. I opened the backpack and pulled out my math book. The three-page assignment was inside of it.

Jennifer kicked my chair from behind. "It was nice knowing you," she laughed. Tracy laughed with her from the desk on my right side. Amanda shook her head. I waited for Vanessa to laugh on my left side, but she wasn't there. The math army was a soldier short.

"Welcome to class," Miss Turner said from the front of the room. "I hope you all had a chance to complete your math assignment." Several kids groaned. "I've got a video for you to watch while I grade them." She pointed to a TV on a cart by her side. "Go ahead and pass your papers forward, please."

Jennifer kicked my chair again. "Here you go," she said. "Don't count the papers. It'll take you all day." She shoved her papers against my arm. I turned and grabbed them. I knew there were only three pages.

Miss Turner was standing over my desk when I turned back around. "I'll take those." I gulped and handed them to her. She looked at them. "Where are your papers, Melissa?"

I stared at my math book. The papers were inside. All I had to do was pull them out and hand them to her. She would never know a cat had done the work. I could get away with it if I wanted to.

But I couldn't do it. I was scared and ashamed when I looked into Miss Turner's eyes. I took a deep breath so I could speak. "I don't have it."

Jennifer jumped out of her seat and stood up. "I did my work, Miss Turner," she said. "It was hard but smart people like me can do it." She looked at me and shook her head like she felt sorry for me. "It's not Melissa's fault she's not smart. She was born that way."

My hands were shaking. I wanted to cry. Miss Turner's face was redder than mine. "Jennifer, get your things and sit by my desk." That's where she made us sit whenever we were in trouble. "What you said was mean and hurtful. Apologize to Melissa right now."

She huffed and said, "I'm sorry you're not any good at math."

Miss Turner guided Jennifer to the desk by hers. She straightened her clothes and came back to my desk. "I'm sorry about that, Melissa. None of what she said is true. I'm going to speak with her parents."

All the kids in that room were staring at me. I had never been so embarrassed in my life. There was only one thing I could do to save myself. I opened the math book and pulled out the three pages. I handed them to Miss Turner. "I thought I forgot them, but here they are."

She looked over the papers and smiled at me. "Thank you, Melissa. I knew you could do it." I sank into my chair when she collected the other papers. *What had I done?*

Miss Turner turned the TV on and played a boring movie about the history of math. At least it was better than doing schoolwork. The people it spoke about had weird names, like Archimedes and Pythagoras. The only name I recognized was Albert Einstein. I think he invented the light bulb. Or was that some other guy?

Miss Turner smiled and winked at me when she sat back down at her desk. I hoped my papers were the last ones she would grade. PJ had probably made up the answers. I crossed my arms over my desk and put my head down. I just wanted the class to end. The anticipation was too much.

"Melissa!" Miss Turner called out from her desk. I looked up at her. My heart beat a million times a minute. She had figured everything out. "Come here for a moment, please."

Tracy chuckled when I stood up. Several boys shouted "ooh" like I was in trouble. My head was spinning. I focused on Miss Turner's desk and took one step at a time toward it.

"Did you have any help with this?" Miss Turner asked when I stood next to her. She was tapping her red marker on my papers.

My lips felt like they were stuck together. My tongue felt like a big ball of cotton in my mouth. "Yes," I finally said. That wasn't a lie. PJ had helped me by doing the whole thing. "I asked my sister for help." That also wasn't a lie.

She stopped tapping her marker. "I have to ask – did your sister do any of this work?" Her lips were as red and as straight as her marker. My sister had been in the class years ago. She had barely passed the class.

I looked Miss Turner straight in the eyes. "My sister

didn't do any of the work. She didn't help me at all."

Miss Turner looked down at my papers again and grunted. She seemed angry at me. It was my fault I hadn't studied harder. I should have asked my dad for help when he was here. "I see," she said. She sounded disappointed. "Go sit back down, please."

Jennifer chuckled from the other side of Miss Turner's desk. I forgot she was there and hadn't noticed her. The leader of the math army had figured I wasn't any good at math. She had heard everything and now she knew it for sure.

I wanted to cry when I walked back to my desk. It was obvious the answers were wrong. I was about to fail this class, and I had never failed anything before. Why did math have to be so hard?

The TV was talking about a guy named Isaac Newton. Whoever he was. I put my head down on my desk again. My life was over. My daddy was going to come home from Puerto Rico and find out I wasn't the smartest girl in the world like he thought I was.

Thirty minutes later, Miss Turner turned the TV off. I sat up straight and stared at the chalkboard behind her. I couldn't look her in the eyes anymore. I felt ashamed. "Most of you did well," Miss Turner said. "One or two of you will need some extra help."

Jennifer made a fake coughing sound. Then she said my name fast and fake coughed again. The whole class laughed.

"Quiet down," Miss Turner said. Her face was red again. "A few of you got a perfect score." Jennifer and Tracy both cheered. They always got perfect scores. "But only one person got the bonus question right."

Jennifer stood up behind Miss Turner. She was all smiles. She waved at the class like she was accepting an award for being the smartest person alive. I felt sick. I couldn't watch her gloat while my life was falling apart. I had to get out of that room.

"That person," Miss Turner said, sounding chipper, "is Melissa." She smiled at me and nodded her approval. The room became silent. No one believed it. How was this possible? I couldn't move.

Jennifer's smile disappeared. Her eyes were so big that they looked like they were going to explode. She sat back down and didn't take her huge eyes off me.

The class bell rang. The kids around me rushed out of the classroom. I would have run out with them, but Miss Turner blocked my way. She looked back and forth from Jennifer to Tracy and Amanda.

"I know it's short notice," Miss Turner said to me, "but the Mathletes could use your help tonight."

Jennifer shot out of her seat. "No!" Her hands were on her hips. Her eyes were redder than a hot volcano.

"Vanessa is sick," Miss Turner said. "The county championship is tonight. You can't play without a fourth person." Jennifer kept shaking her head. "It's not what anyone planned for, but it's the only way you can play."

Why wasn't anyone talking to me about it? The girls didn't want me on the team and I didn't want to be on it. I wasn't any good at math! "I don't think I can make it," I said. "My dad is in Puerto Rico." My sister or Miss Johnson could take me, but they didn't need to know that. I put my math book into my backpack and stood to leave.

"I understand," Miss Turner said. "But you need a few more points to pass this class." She put a hand on my shoulder. "I'll award those points to you if you participate in the competition."

I bit my lower lip. I couldn't fail this class – not now. I'd have to stand next to Jennifer, Tracy, and Amanda and keep my mouth shut. I hated it but what else could I do? "What time does the competition start?"

# FRIDAY AFTERNOON

I held my breath when I knocked on Joe's door again after school. I couldn't believe I had agreed to be a part of the math competition. What was I thinking? I hoped Joe was home so he could give me some tips.

Miss Johnson answered the door. "Hey, Melissa," she said, smiling. "Come on in." She waved for me to join her inside the house. I was glad to see her, but disappointed Joe wasn't there. She must have gotten off from work early for the weekend.

"I've got you now," PJ said from the living room. He was circling slowly around a pink ball of yarn. I shook my head. He pounced on the yarn then batted it away. "Get back here!" he yelled. The yarn unraveled as it rolled down the hallway. He chased after it and pounced on it again.

"It never gets old," Miss Johnson said, chuckling. "Come with me to the kitchen, Melissa. I made chocolate chip cookies." She didn't have to tell me twice. I loved cookies. Chocolate chip was my favorite.

"Joe's not here?" I asked.

She shook her head and told me to take a seat at the kitchen counter. She put a plate of cookies and a glass of milk in front of me. "Joe will be back Sunday night. He's staying with his friend Shane for the weekend." She paused. "And Dana is with her dad."

I felt lost. The cookies smelled great, but I couldn't eat any of them. My stomach was twisted in knots. In a few hours I was supposed to be in a competition I knew nothing about.

"Is everything okay?" Miss Johnson asked. She sat in the chair next to mine and wrapped an arm around me. Her eyes were wide like she was concerned. "You can talk to me."

She was a great mother to Joe and a great aunt to Dana. I could trust her, but I couldn't tell her everything. I couldn't tell anyone everything. "I have a friend who didn't tell the truth about something."

"I see," Miss Johnson said. "And how does your friend feel about this?"

"She's scared and confused," I replied. It felt weird talking about myself like I was someone else. I hoped she didn't realize I was talking about me. "Now she's got to do something she's not comfortable with to cover up her lie."

Miss Johnson took her arm from around me and looked me straight in the eyes. "I don't know what your friend lied about, but I think she'd feel a lot better if she told the truth."

I huffed when she said that. "Everyone will laugh at her if they find out what she did." They would all know I wasn't any good at math. I was so bad at it that a cat had to do it for me!

"Are you going to eat any of those?" she asked, pointing at my cookies. I shook my head. I lost my appetite when I thought about the Mathletes. She stood, grabbed the plate of cookies, and covered them with plastic wrapping. "Tell your friend not to worry about everyone else. It's important she feels good about herself."

She sat back down next to me. "The problem with lies is that you often have to tell more lies to cover the first one up. Then you tell so many that you can't remember what the first one was." She nodded slowly at me, like she wanted to make sure I understood what she was saying. "In the end, you're only hurting yourself. And you may lose the trust of the people you lied to."

She was right. I think she knew I was talking about myself. Joe was lucky to have her as a mom. "Thank you," I whispered. My throat was tight.

PJ walked into the kitchen on his hind legs. His head was as high as my stomach. "That yarn won't bother you anymore," he said to us. "I took care of it. You're welcome."

Miss Johnson reached over and rubbed his head. "You must be starving. Are you ready for your Meow Masters?" She stood and walked over to the kitchen sink. She opened the cabinet beneath it and pulled out a bag of cat food.

PJ jumped up and down. He kept licking his lips. "You know what I like!" he shouted. "Give it to me!" I had to laugh. He could eat whatever he wanted. PJ was addicted to Meow Masters.

He got down on all four paws when Miss Johnson put a bowl of it in front of him. PJ shoved his face into the bowl. He ate it so fast that food went flying all over the floor. When he was done, he burped the way that only a cat can. It sounded like he was coughing up a hairball. A nasty, wet hairball. He wiped his lips with a front paw.

"Mind your manners," Miss Johnson scolded him.

He stood and apologized. He put a paw on my leg. "I

want to be a Meow Master. That would be the life." He was talking about the cat food commercials on TV. The Meow Masters were cats that could do the impossible. They were like ninjas. They could catch balls of light.

PJ scratched at my leg. "Did I win the math game?"

"What math game?" Miss Johnson asked.

I stood and said, "Look at the time. I need to get home."

Miss Johnson handed me the plate of cookies. "Take these with you." She walked with me to the front door. "Your friend sounds like a smart girl. I'm sure she'll do the right thing."

I hugged her. "She will."

PJ scratched at my leg again. "Did I win?"

I looked down at him and smiled. "We both won."

# LATE FRIDAY AFTERNOON

I was surprised to see my sister Angie when I got home. She had never been home this early. "What are you doing here?"

"I've got a surprise for you," she said with a huge smile. She looked excited. I had to stop her. When she got excited, it was hard to get her to stop talking. I had to make her understand the truth about my math problem.

"Hold on to that thought," I told her. "They want me to compete in a math contest tonight."

My sister's eyes got big. "The school?"

I nodded at her. "I'm not going to do it, though." On the way home, I had decided not to go to the math competition. It was dishonest, and I would look like a fool.

Angie grabbed my shoulders. "You have to do it!" She looked like she was out of breath. "No Morgan girl has ever been able to do that." She hugged me. It was awkward because she hadn't hugged me in years.

I pulled away from her. "Daddy doesn't need to know anything about this." I was already going to be in enough trouble when I told Miss Turner the truth on Monday. "Just leave it alone." I had to put this fire out before it started.

Angie put her hands in the air like she was surrendering to the police. "What's wrong, sis?"

I could only shake my head at her. I wanted to cry. I didn't have any problem telling her the truth. I didn't want to have to face my daddy. I couldn't bear the thought of him being disappointed in me.

"Don't be mad at me," she said, "but I called him last night and told him about your math assignment." I couldn't breathe. On most days we couldn't reach him in Puerto Rico. "I'm proud of you. I knew he would be too." She put her hands down.

I had never felt so guilty in my life. Daddy was proud of me for something I didn't do.

"So you see," Angie continued, "you have to go to the math competition." She was smiling again. "We're both proud of you."

I put my hands in my pockets. My head was spinning. I

could go to the competition. It was only for one night. I would let Jennifer and her math army answer the questions. Then all of this could go away. I would never have to lie again, and no one would get hurt.

"It's at the school gym in a couple of hours," I said. I felt exhausted. "You can drop me off."

"Yea!" she squealed. "We're the Morgan sisters. I'll be with you every step of the way." She danced around the room like she had just received the best news in the world.

I shook my head and sighed as I watched her excitement. I was sure no one would be at the gym to watch the competition. There was nothing to worry about. Tonight wouldn't be bad. I just wanted it to be over.

# FRIDAY NIGHT

I froze when I walked into the school gym with Angie by my side. The bleachers were full of parents, grandparents and people I had never seen before. They stared at me. I was sure they were secretly laughing and pointing at me. It was my worst nightmare.

Joe's mother called my name and stood up from the bleachers. She smiled, waved, and walked toward me. I turned to Angie. "How did she know I was here?"

Angie shrugged. "It's because I called her and told her about tonight. You spend a lot of time at her house. I thought it would make you happy."

I jumped when Miss Johnson tapped me on the shoulder. "Hey, Melissa," she said. She looked around the gym and at the tables that were set up in the middle of it. "Does this have anything to do with the math game PJ asked about?"

I wasn't sure what to say to her. I couldn't think

straight with all the noise around me. Everyone was talking. All I could focus on were the tables. Two long wooden tables were laid out straight in the middle of the gym. Four chairs were under each table.

"Did you talk to your friend about her lie?" Miss Johnson asked. She was staring into my eyes. I had never felt so guilty in my life. My stomach felt like it had been punched.

"Welcome to the Covington County Math Competition," a man's voice said through the speakers in the gym. "Contestants, please take your seats."

I wanted to throw up. Miss Johnson smiled at me, nodded, and headed back to the bleachers. "You're going to do great," Angie said to me. "Smile!" A bright light flashed in my face when she took a picture from her cell phone.

I was shocked when Amanda came from behind me and linked her arm around mine. "Come on," my friend said. She pulled me toward the tables. "I'll tell you how this works." I didn't have any choice but to follow her.

When we sat at the table, we were facing the crowd in the bleachers. There must have been hundreds of people. It wasn't supposed to be like that. "I didn't think anyone came to these competitions," I said to Angie.

"It's usually just the parents," she said. "But this is the biggest competition of the year." She looked around me to the table lined up with ours. On the other end were four kids I didn't know. "They're from the Catholic school, Saint Gertrude's."

Jennifer and the rest of her army sat on the other side

of me. "I see you decided to show your face," she said. "Stay out of my way." She rolled her eyes and flipped her hair right into my eyes.

"Here's how it works," Amanda continued. "There's a red buzzer in front of us." I looked at the table before me. There was a red buzzer for each contestant. A sheet of paper and a pencil was next to each buzzer. "If you know the answer when the moderator asks it, press the button. You can calculate on that paper if you don't know right away."

I had a feeling I wouldn't be pressing the button at all. The only things I'd be drawing on the paper were unicorns. I like unicorns. "What if I don't know the answer?"

Amanda laughed. "That's not a problem. Jennifer answers all the questions on this team." That didn't seem right or fair, but who was I to argue? "The first team to get ten points wins."

I looked into the audience and smiled. Everything was going to be okay. I could sit there and act like I knew what I was doing. No one would ever know any different because Jennifer would do all the work. I would pass Miss

Turner's math class. Nothing could go wrong.

"Hey, sis!" Angie called out from behind me. I hadn't realized she never sat in the bleachers. "Before we left home, I told you I had a surprise planned."

I turned to tell her to sit down. I didn't need her embarrassing me in front of all these people. But that's not what happened. The one man I would have never expected to be there was facing me.

"Daddy," I squealed. I jumped out of my seat and ran to hug him. I was full of mixed emotions. I was happy he was back from Puerto Rico. But I felt horrible that he would see me behaving dishonestly.

"I love you, baby girl," he said. "I'm so proud of what you've done." He looked at the table and into the crowd. "Now go show everyone what you can do."

I stumbled back to my seat. My daddy had a huge smile as he sat on the first row of the bleachers with Angie. He gave me a big thumbs up. Seeing Daddy there made me feel like the worst person in the world. There's no way that night could get any worse.

"Is everyone ready?" the same voice I heard on the speakers asked. A man in a black suit was standing at the center of the tables, between the two teams. He spoke to the audience. "For the first time ever, this math competition will be broadcast live on Channel 9."

A woman with a huge TV camera stood right in front of me. I couldn't move a muscle. My face felt like it was cemented in place. I didn't want to be famous — not like this! The woman walked past me and filmed the other contestants.

"The team that wins tonight will be declared the county champions," the moderator continued. "That team will move on to the state championship." He cleared his throat. "Here is the first question: If three out of five teachers gave you homework today, what percent of teachers didn't give you homework?"

Before I could even think about it, Jennifer hit her buzzer. How was that possible? She stood and faced the crowd, though I don't think she was supposed to. "If three out of five teachers gave us homework, then forty percent of them are awesome and didn't give us homework."

The moderator cleared his throat. He looked as surprised as me. There was no way Jennifer could have gotten the answer right. Not that fast. "That's, uh, that's correct. One point for Waterfalls Middle School!" That was the name of our school.

Jennifer waved to the crowd like she was a princess. She made sure to smile big for the TV camera. She sat back down and said to me, "That's how you do math." It didn't look like she had done any math at all.

"Here is tonight's second question," the moderator said. I grabbed my pencil and prepared to draw a unicorn. "If you double the number of books in your locker and add five more, you'll have twenty-three books. How many books do you have in your locker?"

I had three books in my locker. And the latest edition of *Girl's World Magazine*. I had a feeling that wasn't the answer he was looking for.

A boy from the other team hit his buzzer. Jennifer looked around me and glared at the kid at the far end of the table. He wore big green glasses and a green bowtie. He stood with his mouth opened wide. He looked like he was going to pee in his pants.

"If I have twenty-three books then I need to subtract the five that were added," he said. "That gives me eighteen. Since the number was doubled, I need to take away half of that." He stood and stared back at Jennifer with confidence. "I have nine books in my locker." He put his arms in the air. "Boo-yeah!"

Amanda nudged me. "He's cute," she whispered.

"That's correct," the moderator said. "One point for Saint Gertrude's!" He looked directly into the camera. "Ladies and gentlemen, we officially have a math war." The crowd in the bleachers cheered. Jennifer crossed her arms and sat back. I got the feeling no one had ever challenged her. I smiled.

The next hour was exhausting. Jennifer would get an answer right. Then the kid on the other team would get an answer right. It went back and forth like a seesaw. I didn't think it would ever end. The front and back of my paper was full of unicorns.

"It's a tie!" the moderator shouted. "Both teams have nine points. Whichever team answers the next question correctly first, wins!" He grabbed a glass of water and swallowed it all in one gulp. He wiped his brow like this was exciting and exhausting. I didn't care. I was trying to figure out how to tell my dad the truth about everything when this was over.

"The final question is: What is the total number of times that the hour hand, minute hand, and second hand go around a circular clock in one day?"

A buzzer on my team's side went off first. A buzzer on the other team's was right behind it. That team groaned. Jennifer's math army cheered and crowded around me. I had no idea why. But then I did.

The buzzer in front of me was lit up like I had hit it. But I didn't. Jennifer's hand was on it. "What did you do?" I asked her. Why would she destroy the team's chances when she knew I wasn't any good at math?

"I was wrong," she said. "We need you here." The

other girls agreed with her. "The final question is the same one that was on Miss Turner's math assignment as a bonus. You're the only one who got it right." She put her hand over mine. "Let's win this."

Amanda chanted my name softly. "Melissa, Melissa, Melissa." Then the other girls joined her. ""Melissa, Melissa, Melissa." My dad and sister stood from the audience and chanted with them. "Melissa, Melissa, Melissa." Then everything fell apart. More than half of the people in the bleachers chanted my name over and over. "Melissa, Melissa, Melissa." It was deafening.

My whole body shook. I couldn't think. The TV camera pointed at the people cheering for me. Then it focused on me. I had no idea what to say. I had no idea what the answer was.

"We need an answer," the moderator said, "or Saint Gertrude's will have the chance to steal."

I tried to remember the answer I had seen on the math assignment after PJ filled it in. I could only think of one number. "The answer is four."

The moderator sounded excited. "That's…" He shuffled through the papers in his hands, like he was looking at the wrong one. His voice deepened. "That's incorrect."

The cheering stopped. The room fell silent. Except for a cricket. A cricket chirped somewhere in the gym and wouldn't stop. I waved the camera away and put my hands over my face.

"I knew you were a fraud," Jennifer spat at me. "You're going to pay for this."

The moderator leaned over and whispered, "Sorry, kid." Then he stood up straight and talked to the camera. "And now for the nail-biting climax. Saint Gertrude's, what is your answer?"

The kid at the end of the table stood again. He was shorter than I thought he was. And he was cute like Amanda said. "The hour hand goes around the clock two times every twenty-four hours. The minute hand goes around twenty-four times. And the second hand goes around 1440 times." He smiled big and pointed at Jennifer. "The correct answer is 1466. Boo-yeah!"

"That's correct!" the moderator shouted. "Saint Gertrude's wins!"

Half of the audience cheered. Jennifer and her math army stood, shook their heads at me, and stormed away from the table. Amanda wouldn't look at me. I grabbed her hand as she walked by.

"I could use a friend right now," I told her. She had been my friend when the other girls weren't. I would forever be known as the girl at school who lost the math championship. My dad and sister had believed I was someone that I wasn't. I was scared and lost. It was all my fault.

"I don't understand," Amanda said, pulling her hand away from me. "You knew the answer, but you blew it."

Miss Johnson stepped out of the bleachers, nodded at me kindly, and left the gym. I should have listened to her. Maybe I could save my friendship with Amanda. I had to tell her the truth.

"I didn't know the answer," I admitted. I watched her eyes to see how she would react when I told her about PJ. "My cat did my math homework."

It was at that very moment I realized the TV camera was pointed directly at me. The woman behind the camera lowered it when I said that. She looked confused and amazed. I stepped over to her. "You can't show that on TV."

"Sorry, kid," she said. "This is live TV."

I rubbed my eyes and put my hands on my head. No one was supposed to know about PJ. It had caused too much trouble when people found out Fox could walk and talk. Maybe it was okay. I didn't really have a cat. I liked to think of him as mine.

I turned back to Amanda, but she was gone. She was at the table with the winning team, talking to the boy who had been nervous at first but was confident when he got the answers right. I was afraid I had lost my friend forever.

I took a deep breath as my dad and Angie approached me. They would tell me that they were proud of me because I had at least tried. But I wasn't sure what they would tell me when I explained to them how I got here. I smiled at them, prepared for my whole world to collapse.

# LATE FRIDAY NIGHT

I had a heart attack when I got home with my daddy and Angie. We went in the front door, turned the lights on, and a bunch of people shouted at us, "Surprise!"

Daddy held Angie and me back to protect us. But then he put a hand on his chest and laughed. "You guys!" he shouted. I recognized the Hunters and a few of Daddy's friends. Miss Johnson was there too. Now I knew why she had left the gym in such a hurry.

They crowded around my dad and said things like, "Welcome home!" and "Good to see you!" It took me a moment to realize this was a party for Daddy. He had been in Puerto Rico for months. I shook my head at Angie. No doubt she had planned this.

"Sorry you didn't win tonight," Miss Johnson said to me when she broke away from the crowd. Everyone else was listening to my dad tell stories about his time in Puerto Rico. "But at least you tried."

I wanted to tell her that I hadn't tried. I owed her that much because she had warned me what could happen if I lied and continued to lie. I had to explain it wasn't a friend that needed help — it was me. I took a deep breath and cleared my throat.

"Speech, speech, speech, speech!" Mr. Hunter shouted. He was an old guy with a bald head and long curly mustache and bushy eyebrows. A lot of kids thought he looked scary, but he was sweet. Miss Johnson turned to face him and shook her head. He was holding up a cocktail glass. All the adults had one.

Daddy held out a hand for Mr. Hunter to hush. "Alright now," he said, chuckling. "I'm happy to be back home with my family and friends. I was given the opportunity to help some of the people in Puerto Rico. They didn't have electricity and couldn't enjoy what we do every day. Some of them are still in trouble. I don't deserve praise. It's our responsibility to help each other."

"Hear, hear!" Mr. Hunter shouted. The adults raised their glasses.

Daddy put out a hand again. "There is one person in this room who deserves praise." He scanned the room until he locked eyes with me. "My daughter Melissa – the math genius!"

They stared at me. The room felt like it was caving in. They smiled and waved their glasses at me. I thought I was going to pass out.

"Wait," I said. I couldn't do this anymore. Daddy had to know the truth. "Daddy, I'm not a math genius." The lights were so bright they were blinding me. "I'm failing my math class and I cheated on my test."

The room fell silent. Mrs. Hunter grabbed her husband's shoulder and said, "It's time to go, dear. Let's let them talk about this." She nodded at me and pulled him along. The others in the room said their goodbyes.

I turned to Miss Johnson to apologize to her, but she was gone. I hoped she didn't leave because of me. I looked back at Daddy and Angie. He looked confused and hurt.

"I don't understand," Daddy said. "You're on the math team and you were in the competition. What's going on?"

I did my best not to cry. "I'm sorry, Daddy. Please don't be mad." My hands were shaking. He had always taught me to be honest. I couldn't tell him a cat had done my homework. That would make me look like a bigger liar. "I'm not good at math. I don't understand it. A friend did my homework for me."

His face was blank. It looked like the life was sucked out of it. He told me the one thing that hurt more than him being mad at me. "I'm not mad. Just disappointed."

That's when I cried. He came to me and wrapped his arms around me. "This too will pass," he said. "I don't want you to feel lost. We'll find you a math tutor." He put his hands on my shoulders and made sure I was looking at him. "I'm not disappointed about the math. I'm disappointed you lied."

Angie stood next to us. "I hate to leave but I've got a date." I could tell she was uncomfortable with me crying. I wondered if she really had a date. Daddy nodded at her.

"Thank you for telling me the truth tonight," he said to me. "Tomorrow you must tell the truth to everyone you lied to." Two more people needed to know. One was Miss Johnson. The other was my math teacher Miss Turner but she'd have to wait until Monday. The twisting and churning in my stomach wouldn't stop.

# SATURDAY MORNING

I kicked a rock across the dirt road as I walked towards Joe's house. My math assignment was in my right hand. I had told Daddy the truth about how I aced it. He was disappointed I had cheated but was proud of me for telling the truth. Now he wanted me to tell Miss Johnson the truth. I hoped I could catch her before she went to the farmers market.

I froze when I got close to the yard. News vans were parked all over the dirt and grass. One was for local Channel 9. The others were national news services.

I ran into the yard. Miss Johnson didn't want anyone to know about PJ. The reporters had to be here because of PJ, but I had no idea how they knew he was here. This was all my fault. I had to do something.

Reporters and camera people stood in front of the

house. Miss Johnson stood in the doorway, facing them. She was silent as they kept asking her questions like, "Is it true? Can the cat do math?"

Miss Johnson motioned for me to come into the house. I was behind the reporters and cameramen and would have to squeeze between them. They turned and looked at me.

I felt sick when I saw a man who looked like Chen, the most wanted man in America. The FBI had taken him away when he threatened Fox and put us all in danger. He was the main reason Fox had left. When the man saw me, he pulled a cap over his eyes and walked away.

"Hey, that's the girl!" one of the reporters shouted. They crowded around me like cereal in a box. They asked so many questions so fast that I couldn't understand anything. I wanted to scream for help.

Miss Johnson reached through the crowd, grabbed my hand, and pulled me to the front door. "Back off, vultures!" I stood behind her and shivered. "She's just a kid!"

"We've all seen the video of the talking fox," a female reporter in a red dress said. It had been all over the internet. "Is there a cat here that can do the same thing?" A bunch of microphones were shoved in front of us.

"No comment," Miss Johnson said. "I want you off my property right now." She crossed her arms. "Don't make me call the police."

A few of them grunted. The microphones disappeared. "Let's go," the female reporter shouted to the crew with her. "Just another false lead." They turned and headed back to their vans.

"Hey!" Miss Johnson shouted at the reporter. "Who told you there was a cat here that could do math?"

The reporter shrugged. "It was an anonymous tip." She shook her head and frowned. I felt bad for her because the tip was right. But who else knew PJ was here? And why would they do that?

Miss Johnson started to shut the door, but a man called out, "Hang on there just a second." He wore a gray suit with a blue tie. He smiled big, holding a briefcase in one hand and a hat in the other. He didn't look like the other reporters.

"I tried to be nice," Miss Johnson said. "You reporters are not welcome here. Get off my land."

He held out his hands and stepped closer to the front door. "I'm not a reporter." He reached into a pocket on the front of his shirt and pulled out a card. "My name is Jason Peters. I represent Meow Masters cat food."

PJ appeared out of nowhere. He brushed past me on four paws and stood next to Miss Johnson. He looked up at Mr. Peters and meowed when Miss Johnson took his card.

"I know this is a stressful time with the media," Mr. Peters said. "But I can help."

Miss Johnson read his card. She uncrossed her arms. "How can you help?"

He smiled. "Meow Masters gets its success from cats that do impossible things." He winked at PJ. "I'll let you in on a secret." He looked around to make sure the reporters were gone. "None of it's true," he whispered.

I chuckled. Everyone knew the cats couldn't really do what they did on the commercials. They couldn't fly. They couldn't brush their teeth. And they couldn't catch balls of light.

"Everyone thinks this cat can do math... let them think that!" He waved his arms like he was excited. "We'll put your cat in his own commercial. It's good TV."

Miss Johnson handed his card back to him. "I'm not sure it's a good idea. Thank you, though." PJ meowed loudly and hit her leg with a paw.

Mr. Peters grunted and put the card back into his pocket. "That's a shame." He looked down at PJ. "I could have made you a star, little guy. And you would have had a lifetime supply of Meow Masters." Mr. Peters' eyes got big after what happened next.

PJ looked back at me and then up at Miss Johnson. His eyes glossed over when he stared at Mr. Peters next. He slowly stood up on his two hind legs and said, "When can I start?"

# SATURDAY AFTERNOON

"Dana and her father are coming over," Miss Johnson told me. "My brother is concerned."

Mr. Mike was a good guy. He loved to watch wrestling and made sure we were all taken care of.

"What do you have there?" Miss Johnson asked, pointing at the papers in my hand. I forgot I had them. I didn't want to tell her the truth, but I owed it to her.

"This is a math assignment I had." We walked into the kitchen. She turned the oven on. "Remember that I told you about my friend? The one who told a lie?"

She rubbed her chin. "Yeah. Did she get a chance to tell the truth?"

I shrugged. "Not to everyone." I took a deep breath. "I don't have a friend who lied. It was me." I held up the papers. "I didn't do this homework. PJ did."

She looked behind me at PJ as he walked into the kitchen. "You can do homework?" she asked him. She acted surprised, but she winked at me. "You can't even use a litter box."

"It's not my fault," PJ complained. "You try pooping on litter. I'd rather dig a hole out back." I couldn't stop laughing. PJ insisted on going outside like a dog. He had been a stray cat when he found this home. It wasn't so bad.

He helped keep the grass green.

"I want to do the commercial," PJ said. "Being a Meow Master is my destiny."

Someone knocked on the front door. "That better not be another reporter," Miss Johnson said. She turned the oven off. She walked out of the kitchen and through the living room towards the front door.

"You're okay if I go?" PJ asked, walking alongside Miss Johnson. "I'll get you a front row seat to all the action." He was purring. "I won't forget you when I'm famous."

Miss Johnson stopped walking. "Listen to me, PJ." She sounded exhausted. "I know you want to do it, but it's not safe." She patted his head.

PJ didn't say anything when she continued walking. I wasn't sure if he was mad or sad. He walked away slowly on all four paws. His tail was between his legs.

"Come on in," Miss Johnson said after she opened the door. "Where's your key?" Mr. Mike and Dana came inside. Mr. Mike had on a pair of shorts and a tank top. He looked like he just rolled out of bed.

"I don't know," Mr. Mike said. "Maybe your cat ate it." He smirked. "Look who we dragged in with us." He used his thumb to point behind him. He headed for the couch and turned the TV on. The Native Indian Elan smiled big when he walked in. He was the last member of The Talking Dragon tribe. I hadn't seen him since the night he helped set Fox free to return to his parents.

"I'm happy to see you all again," he said. He was handsome with his short hair and bronze skin. He had his satchel and laptop with him. "I heard rumors about a cat doing math. Is he here?"

"PJ!" Miss Johnson yelled.

Dana stood by my side and shuddered. "I hate it when she does that." I agreed. Nothing is scarier than an adult yelling your name.

"You changed your mind?" PJ asked when he raced into the room on his hind legs. He covered his mouth when he saw Elan. "I remember you," he said. "You were there the night I first talked."

Elan bent down so he was the same height as PJ. "It amazes me how spectacular you are. You walk and talk like you've been doing it your entire life. And now you're a math genius?"

PJ looked over at Miss Johnson. "I like this guy. He knows what he's talking about." His eyes got big and watery. He was cute when he did that. "I'm spectacular — like a Meow Master."

"You're not going," Miss Johnson repeated. PJ's eyes went back to their regular size and dryness.

"Meow Master?" Elan asked, standing back up.

"It's a cat food commercial," she replied. She shook her head with every word. "They want PJ to talk and do math in it."

"You're gonna be famous!" Dana squealed.

Elan stood by Miss Johnson's side. "You can't do that," he said to PJ. "Something has changed with this land. It was silent for hundreds of years." He looked at each of us. "First there was a talking fox. Now there's a talking cat." He put a hand on Miss Johnson's shoulder. "And a boy who's stronger and smarter than all of us."

He was talking about Joe. I remembered when Joe did

57

twenty pull-ups in P.E. class. No one thought he could do more than one.

"Don't forget about the chicken," Dana said. Joe was the only person who had heard Old Nelly speak. His great grandma claimed to have talked to her for years. She claimed Old Nelly could lay golden eggs. The whole town knew Old Nelly could only lay rotten eggs.

"I didn't know why this land gave them power," Elan continued. "I didn't know what it had chosen them for."

"What?" PJ asked. "What did it choose me for?"

Elan winked at him. "I believe you were chosen to protect this land."

"From what?" Dana asked.

Elan shrugged. "I don't know yet. I fear something dark is coming."

That reminded me of the man with the cap. I stood in front of Miss Johnson to get her attention. "I saw a man when we were outside with the reporters. He looked like the man who wanted to take Fox to China."

Mr. Mike stood from the couch and faced me. "Chen? You saw Chen?" His face was red.

"I don't know," I admitted. "Maybe." He looked like Chen, but he had a cap on. He pulled it over his eyes and left before I could confirm it. I bit my lower lip. "The reporters surrounded me."

"This is bad," Mr. Mike said. He walked around the couch and stood by my side. "Real bad. We need a plan."

Miss Johnson stood in front of us. "Everyone calm down. We all saw Chen get taken away by the FBI." She nodded her head slowly again to make sure we understood every word. "There's no way it could have been him. He's in prison for the rest of his life."

Mr. Mike's face was still red. "You remember what he wanted to do to Fox? He wanted to take him apart piece by piece." He looked down at PJ. "What if he wants to do the same thing to the cat?"

PJ cleared his throat. "Wait a minute. You're saying this wacko may be in town? I'm going to hide in the litter box."

"Shane got a card from that FBI guy, didn't he?" Mr. Mike asked. "After he helped him catch Chen?" I nodded. Shane made sure he contacted the FBI when Chen was here the last time. "We can get in touch with him and clear all of this up." One of the agents had been impressed with Shane and left a card with him for a job when he got older.

"It's settled," Miss Johnson said. "We'll give Shane a call and see if he's still got that card." She nodded at all of us and smiled.

Elan said his goodbyes. I was sure we would see him again. Mr. Mike tried to call Shane but had to leave a message. PJ hid under the couch. He still wouldn't touch the litter box.

Miss Johnson put her arms around me and Dana. "Try not to worry, girls. I'm sure we'll be fine."

I wish she had been right.

# SUNDAY MORNING

I sat in the back row of church because that's where
Joe always sat. Angie and my dad sat with Miss Johnson at
the front. I turned every time I heard someone come
through the foyer, hoping it was Joe.

"He's playing video games," Dana said next to me.
"You know how boys are." I smiled weakly. She knew me
too well. I took a deep breath and faced forward. I wasn't
sure I'd ever see Joe again.

I thought about PJ. I felt bad he couldn't do the
commercial like he wanted to. Instead, he was at Joe's
house with Dana's dad, watching wrestling. PJ didn't
understand wrestling and thought it was silly.

The church organ came to life. I don't know why, but
the organist always played the same song – *How Great Thou
Art*. Her hair was gray, and her fingers were long and bony.
She was the sweetest woman in the world. No one ever
complained about the song.

"Brothers and sisters," the preacher said from the front
of the church. The choir was seated behind him. "This is
the day that the Lord has made." Several people said
'Amen'. "Let us rejoice and be glad in it." In any other
church, the organist would have played that song then and
there. Not ours. She was eating an apple.

"Proverbs 22 says that the Lord detests lying lips," the preacher continued. The room felt hot at that moment. I was sure the air conditioner was broken.

Someone put their hand on my shoulder. My heart jumped. Was it Chen? I turned and smiled at my best friend. "Joe," I whispered. The land had changed him. He was leaner, and his smile was brighter. He sure was cute.

He smiled and walked around the pew to join me. I panicked because there wasn't anywhere for him to sit. Dana was on my right. Sally was on my left. I didn't know Sally very well, but she was always in trouble at school. She pulled the fire alarm last week.

"Hey, Sally," Dana hissed as she leaned across me. "How many times do I have to tell you? You need Jesus. Go sit up front."

Sally crossed her arms. "I'm tired of you bossing me around. I'm not going anywhere." I cleared my throat, hoping they'd leave each other alone. I could sit anywhere, as long as it was next to Joe.

Dana reached over and pinched Sally's leg. Sally shrieked. Half of the church looked back at us. "Go, go, go," Dana said. Her face was as stern as a rock.

Sally stood and huffed. "You'll pay for this, you little demon." Her voice was broken. I could tell she was in pain. She held her leg and scooted out of the row.

Joe took her place next to me. "Sorry I'm late," he said.

"There's so much to tell you," I replied.

He nodded. "I heard about PJ." He leaned against my arm. "Don't worry. I'm not going to let anything bad happen to him." I knew he meant it. Joe had done everything he could to protect Fox. "Shane has been trying to contact the FBI agent all morning."

"The Lord delights in people who are trustworthy!" the preacher shouted out. "All those who ask for forgiveness and change their ways will receive it."

I turned to Joe. "I needed your help with a math assignment." I didn't want to complain, but he had to know.

"I wasn't trying to avoid you," he assured me. "I feel lost without Fox."

Dana leaned across my lap when the organist played *How Great Thou Art* again. It was time to go. "Kissy, kissy," she teased. She smacked her lips together. Joe and I both blushed.

"Let's go check on PJ," Joe said. He stood and motioned for us to follow him. "He's always getting into trouble."

# SUNDAY AFTERNOON

I went back to Joe's house with his family. Miss Johnson cooked spaghetti on Sundays. I asked her once how she made it. She said she made it with love. And tomato sauce.

Mr. Mike was sitting on the couch, watching wrestling. A big guy named Mr. Awesome Muscles was flexing his muscles on TV. He kept talking about how awesome he was.

"Where's PJ?" Joe asked.

Mr. Mike looked back at us. "Oh, hey." He brushed a hand at us like we were disturbing him. "He had to relieve himself."

Joe shook his head and said, "I'll be right back." If PJ had to use the bathroom, then he was out back somewhere.

"Melissa, come help me with lunch," Miss Johnson said

to me. "We need to chat." I wasn't sure what she wanted to talk about, but she never asked anyone to help her with the spaghetti. It was a secret family recipe handed down from her grandmother.

"What did your father say?" she asked, putting oven mitts on her hands. She opened the oven and slid in a pan with garlic bread on it. "When you told him the truth?"

"He wasn't happy about it," I admitted. I hated seeing the disappointment on his face. "But he was glad I told him the truth." I was glad he heard it from me and not from TV.

"Good," Miss Johnson said. She winked at me. "You can always come to me for help if you need it." I smiled because it was true. She would never judge me and always help me.

"He's not out there," Joe said when he walked in through the back door. "I can't find PJ anywhere." Joe's face was flush. He looked out of breath.

"Maybe he came back in," Miss Johnson said. Her face had creases in it, like she was thinking hard.

"Not a chance," Mr. Mike said, walking into the kitchen. "I've been here the whole time. PJ went out the back door and has not come back."

Miss Johnson ran her hands through her hair. "Shane hasn't heard back from the FBI?" she asked Joe. He shook his head. "I don't know what to think," she continued. "I'm afraid Chen has something to do with this."

"We've got to do something!" Dana cried. "PJ's just a cat. A crazy, stubborn cat."

*"Meow Masters — saving the world one cat at a time,"* a deep

voice said from the TV in the living room. I peeked around the kitchen doorway and saw the Meow Masters commercial playing on TV. A Persian cat was flying in a cape like a superhero. It looked real.

"What about the commercial?" I asked everyone in the room.

"What about it?" Mr. Mike said.

I focused on Miss Johnson. "PJ wanted to make one of those commercials." I pointed to the TV. "What if he actually went to make one?"

"Maybe," Miss Johnson said. "I wouldn't put it past him."

Someone banged on the front door. "Who can that be at a time like this?" Miss Johnson asked. We all walked to the door, discussing what to do about PJ. Dana wanted to lock him in his litter box.

Shane was on the other side of the door when we opened it. "Where's he at?" he asked. He walked past us. "We need to keep PJ in this house."

"What's wrong?" Joe asked.

Shane held out a cell phone. "I got a call from the FBI. Chen escaped last week."

Five minutes later I was in the backseat of Miss Johnson's car with Joe by my side. Miss Johnson was driving, and Shane was in the front passenger seat. Dana stayed at the house with Mr. Mike in case PJ came back.

"He's going to be okay," Joe said to me. "He has to be."

"It's right up here," Shane said, watching the GPS on his cell phone. The FBI had given him the address of the

Meow Masters commercial filming. We didn't know if PJ would be there, but it was our only hope. No one knew how to find Chen.

I looked through the windshield. A big white screen was up ahead outside. PJ was in front of it with a camera crew. A security guard waved us down before we could get any closer.

Miss Johnson rolled her window down. "Is there a problem, officer?"

"You folks need to turn around," he said, tipping his hat. "This is a closed set." He smiled big and pointed at the road behind us.

Miss Johnson turned the car off and took the keys out. "We're not going anywhere." I gulped. Daddy had taught me to obey the police. "Our cat is over there, and he's in danger."

The security guard took his hat off. "Look, ma'am, I don't want any trouble." Sweat covered his forehead. "Turn the car back on and go home."

She looked back at Joe and me. "Open your doors and get out." She opened hers first and stood in front of the guard. Then she cocked her arm back and threw her keys toward the white screen. "Whoops."

"Wait a minute," the guard said. "Do not leave your vehicle. Stay in your seats."

Joe opened his door next. I looked over at my door, but I couldn't get myself to open it. I didn't want to get in trouble for not listening to the guard.

Joe stepped out and reached for my hand. "Come on," he said. "Let's go save that crazy cat." I realized he was right. PJ was in danger and it was our job to protect him. What was there to think about? I grabbed Joe's hand and stepped out.

"Hey, you kids, get back in the car!" the guard shouted. He looked scary. He carried a gun and had handcuffs. He rubbed the sweat off his forehead and threw his hands in the air like he had given up.

"Sorry," I whispered.

He shook his head at me. "Hey," he said. "You're the girl." He smiled for the first time. "The one from TV." His face lit up. "Yeah, you were in the math competition."

I wanted to bury my head. I didn't want to be remembered as the girl who lost the math competition. All I could do was nod.

He rubbed his chin and shrugged. "That cat's a pain in the butt. Go get him."

Joe held onto my hand and pulled me toward the white board. "Let's go." His mom nodded at us. We ran toward the screen and cameras. It wasn't that far. We'd be there in less than a minute.

We passed through two cameramen. PJ was in front of the screen, holding a can of Meow Masters. "Meow," he said, licking his lips. "It's delicious." I never expected what happened next. It changed everything.

"Do it again, you stupid cat!" Jennifer screamed at him. Yes, it was the same Jennifer that was the leader of the math team. The same Jennifer that said I would pay for losing the math competition. How could this be happening?

"Look who's here," she said when she spotted me. "The world's biggest loser." She shook her head and laughed. "Let me tell you what's going on since you're not smart enough to figure it out."

I didn't have time for her games. PJ was in danger and we had to get him out of there. "PJ," I said to him, "let's go. Don't let her treat you like this."

PJ didn't move. "I'm about to be famous." He shook his head. "I can't leave now." He looked at Jennifer. "Let's keep filming."

Jennifer snorted. "You see, he belongs to me now." She smirked and winked at Joe like he belonged to her too. "Did you ever wonder how the reporters found PJ? How Meow Masters found him?" I did, but now I knew.

"Your good friend Amanda told me that you spend a lot of time at Joe's house," she continued. "It doesn't take a genius to figure out where a talking cat could come from. Joe already made the mistake of posting his talking fox all over the internet."

"That wasn't me!" Joe shouted. Shane had recorded the video of Fox talking to Joe, without him knowing about it. That was before they were friends, and Shane was trying to destroy him.

"You two are a cute couple," Jennifer said. "And dumb." She walked over to me and stared into my eyes like she wanted to pick a fight. "I called every news station I could and told them about PJ. Then I struck a deal with Meow Masters. I told them I would get them a cat that could do math, but only if they let me direct the commercial." She smiled like she was proud of herself.

Joe stepped between us and faced Jennifer. "Back off." She laughed and stepped back. "PJ," Joe shouted at him, "Chen is back and he's after you."

Jennifer faced PJ. "Don't listen to them. No one is after you." She walked over to him and petted his head. "They just want to hold you back. I can make sure you get a lifetime supply of Meow Masters. And we'll get you a sports car. Every cat will know your name."

PJ purred. His eyes were frozen, like he was dreaming of all that food and driving his own car. But then his eyes drifted to me. He sighed. "Cats can't drive," he said to Jennifer. "And don't ever talk to my friends like that again." He smiled at me.

That's when I knew everything was going to be okay. We'd take PJ back to Joe's house, protect him, and live happily ever after. But life doesn't always go the way we planned it.

One of the cameramen threw his camera down and rushed toward PJ. I recognized him as the man from China, Chen. He reached for PJ's neck and grabbed him by the scruff. He held PJ up in the air. PJ couldn't move, like he was paralyzed.

Jennifer ran off, screaming.

"Let him go!" Joe shouted. His shoulders were squared, and his fists were out. My heart was racing.

Chen laughed. "There's no one to help you this time." He studied PJ's fur. "I'm going to find out if there really is more than one way to skin a cat."

"No, you're not," Miss Johnson said from behind me. I was happy to hear her voice. Joe could protect me, but no one can protect you more than a mom. "You're going to put the cat down and walk away."

Chen shook his head. "You should leave before you get hurt." He held PJ in front of us like a trophy. "This cat isn't worth it. He's just a mangy animal with a big mouth."

"No," Joe said. "He's family."

Shane appeared behind Chen. We hadn't noticed him in all the commotion. He was holding the camera Chen had thrown down in both hands. "Hey!" he shouted at Chen.

As soon as Chen turned, Shane whacked him across the head with the camera. Chen fell like a chopped tree. PJ fell out of his grip and landed on all four paws. "Don't mess with my friends," Shane said, standing over Chen's body.

The sound of sirens filled the air. Police cars sped down the road toward us. Helicopters hovered over us. Maybe there would be a happy ending after all.

"Thank you," PJ said, standing on his hind legs. He stood between me and Joe. "I don't know what I was thinking." I patted his head.

"We all make mistakes," Miss Johnson said. "That's okay, as long as we learn from them." She smiled at him and nodded her head the way she always did when she wanted to make a point.

"I did learn something," he replied. "I learned it's too dangerous for you to be around me." He stared into the distance. "I'm a stray cat. I'm supposed to be alone — that's what cats do."

"You're my cat!" I cried. "You can't leave." He didn't want to believe he belonged to anyone, but he owned a piece of my heart. I didn't want to lose him.

"The power you have — the power to walk and talk — that comes from our property," Joe said. He sounded sad. His heart had been broken when Fox left. Though he had never bonded with PJ, I didn't think his heart could take much more. "If you leave, you'll become sick and even worse."

Miss Johnson put one arm around me and the other around Joe. She was still behind us. "You're not a danger to us," she said to PJ. "You're a blessing to us. You make our lives better and fill our home with happiness. We smile when you chase lights on the wall and fight with balls of yarn."

PJ smirked. "I am a pretty swell cat. Let's go home."

The FBI took Chen away. They thanked Shane for his assistance. They said he'd make a good agent one day. I could breathe again because PJ was safe. I thought that was end of this. But it was only the beginning.

# SUNDAY NIGHT

Dana hugged PJ as soon as we got back to Joe's house. "Don't ever do that again," she told the cat. The microwave made a beeping sound in the kitchen. Dana darted her eyes at each of us. "Those are my pizza rolls. Nobody touch them."

Mr. Mike waved at us from the couch. He was watching wrestling again. Mr. Awesome Muscles was fighting for a championship belt. "I wish Fox was here," he said. "He would have loved this."

Joe sighed and walked past me into the kitchen. I heard the back door open and close. I suspected he was going to disappear again.

"Hey, Melissa," PJ said, "come check this out." He waved a paw for me to follow him. He led me to the bathroom hallway, where his litter box was at. It was a waste of money. He would never use it. "Look inside," he

said.

It was an unusual request. I didn't want to stick my head inside a dirty litter box. But, it was unused. There was nothing to worry about. I was confused by what I found.

"Hey," I said. "Isn't that my math assignment?" I recognized my name on the front page. The paper was laying on top of the litter. "There were three pages. Where are the other two?"

PJ smirked and said, "You don't want to know." They say curiosity kills a cat. I was curious, but I was a human. I looked deeper into the litter box. Two lumps were buried in the litter. I had a pretty good idea what they were.

"That's disgusting," I said, sticking my tongue out and holding my stomach. I would never look at homework the same way.

"Thank you," he said, smiling. "It's some of my best work." He put a paw on my leg. "And thank you for looking out for me. You are a true friend." I smiled back at him and played with his ears.

Miss Johnson walked into the hallway and joined us. "What are you two so happy about?" she asked. She crossed her arms like she thought we were up to no good.

I winked at PJ. "My cat ate my homework." I burst out laughing with him. It wasn't an excuse. It's what really happened.

Miss Johnson raised her eyebrows like she was confused. "Alright, then," she said. "Melissa, can you go check on Joe? He's asking for you."

I nodded at her. I would do anything for Joe. Miss Johnson thanked me when I walked past her and headed for the back door. I stopped and looked back at PJ.

"Don't worry," he assured me, "I'll be here when you get back." That was what I needed to hear. I walked through the hallway and into the kitchen.

"These are my pizza rolls," Dana said again. "Don't touch them." I shook my head and opened the back door. Dana giggled when I looked back at her. As tough as she was, she was like a baby sister to me. I smiled at her.

I stepped into the backyard and walked past the outhouse. I wondered what I was going to say to Joe. He didn't talk to anyone anymore. Months ago, he had told me that he liked me — really liked me. I later admitted the same thing to him. My stomach was full of butterflies.

I sat next to Joe on the green grass close to the chicken coop. Joe was staring into the woods behind the fence in front of us. This was where we had last seen Fox.

"He's never coming back, is he?" Joe asked. He kept staring into the woods. I wanted to sound positive, but we both knew the answer. Fox had been kidnapped by Shane's dad one time and almost tortured by Chen another time. Now he was back with his parents.

"No," I said, leaning against his shoulder. "But he's safe because of you." I wanted to be honest with him. "Fox gave up his ability to walk and talk so we wouldn't be in danger. It was the right thing to do."

"I'm afraid," Joe said, leaning on my arm now. He was strong and fast. He had nothing to be afraid of. "I heard Elan was here. He said something dark is coming."

We both jumped when the chickens went crazy in the coop. They were distressed and squawked loudly like a predator was attacking them. Joe stood and shouted, "Mom! Help!"

She rushed out of the back door. Dana was behind her with Mr. Mike. "Stand back!" Miss Johnson commanded. "We don't know what's in there. It could be a dangerous animal." We were all scared after what Elan had told us. The chickens cackled, "kuh-kuh-kuh-KACK!"

Miss Johnson slowly stepped into the coop with Mr. Mike. We all followed her, even though she told us to stay back. *Curiosity kills a cat*, I thought again.

I froze when Miss Johnson stopped and put a hand over her mouth. "I don't believe this," she whispered, sounding confused. I came from around her and stood by her side with the others to see what she was talking about.

An animal with brownish orange hair had its back to us. The end of its tail was white. I gasped when it turned to face us. It had the same blue eyes as Joe. I knew right away who it was.

Fox stood slowly on his two hind legs and looked at all of us, one by one. His eyes stopped and focused on Joe. "I heard you were in trouble," he said in his childish voice. "I came back to help."

Discover the origins of Fox to learn how all of this began. My fox isn't like other foxes. He walks on two legs and talks like a human. This is his story. This is his beginning.

AVAILABLE AT AMAZON.COM
Print and Ebook

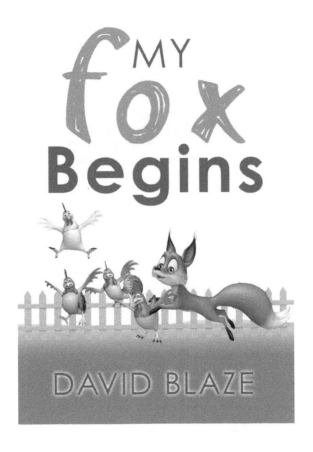

You can keep up with everything I'm doing and get more information about my stories at **www.davidblazebooks.com**

And you can follow me on Facebook at **https://www.facebook.com/davidblazeauthor** . Be sure to like the page so you know what PJ and Fox are up to.

The name David Blaze was envisioned by Timothy David for his son, Zander Blaze, to create a world for him and all children that is fun, safe, enlightening, hilarious, and honest. Wow! That's awesome!

If you enjoyed my story, please tell your friends and family. I'd also appreciate it if you'd leave a review on Amazon.com and tell me what you think about my friend, PJ.

DAVID BLAZE

CPSIA information can be obtained
at www.ICGtesting.com
Printed in the USA
FSHW020554120419
57191FS

9 781732 591455